WENDY MEDDOUR is the author and illustrator of *A Hen in the Wardrobe* and *The Black Cat Detectives* in the *Cinnamon Grove* series for Frances Lincoln. The series has been critically acclaimed, and *A Hen in the Wardrobe* won the John C Laurence Award for writing that improves relations between races. It was shortlisted for the Branford Boase Award for an outstanding first novel and in 2014 was chosen as one of the DIVERSE VOICES top 50 books celebrating cultural diversity. Wendy was brought up in Aberystwyth and spent many years teaching English at Oxford University. She is also the author of the bestselling *Wendy Quill* books and writes and paints from her home in Wiltshire.

REBECCA ASHDOWN was born and brought up by the sea in West Sussex. She studied at Norwich School of Art, Westminster University and Central St Martins, and then worked as a graphic and motion designer, filmmaker and freelance vector artist. She is now concentrating on illustration, and uses drawing, printmaking and digital techniques to create her pictures. *How the Library (not the Prince) Saved Rapunzel* is Rebecca's first children's book. She lives near Stroud, Gloucestershire.

To my brilliant, book-loving friend - Claire Edmeston
W.M.

To all my family and friends
R.A.

JANETTA OTTER-BARRY BOOKS

Text copyright © Wendy Meddour 2014
Illustrations copyright © Rebecca Ashdown 2014
The rights of Wendy Meddour and Rebecca Ashdown to be identified respectively as
the author and illustrator of this work have been asserted by them in accordance
with the Copyright, Designs and Patents Act, 1988 (United Kingdom).

First published in Great Britain and in the USA in 2014 by
Frances Lincoln Children's Books, 74-77 White Lion Street, London N1 4PF
www.franceslincoln.com

First paperback edition published in Great Britain in 2015

A catalogue record for this book is available from the British Library.

ISBN 978-1-84780-662-8
Illustrated digitally
Printed in China

1 3 5 7 9 8 6 4 2

How the Library
(NOT the Prince)
Saved Rapunzel

Frances Lincoln
Children's Books

On the sixteenth floor of a tall tower block
sat Rapunzel, quite idle, whilst growing her locks.

"Rapunzel, Rapunzel, please let down your hair,"

called the milkman from down on the bottom stair.
"The lift is not working, the stairs are too steep,
my asthma is bad and my heart is too weak."

But Rapunzel just sat.
She didn't move.
She had nowhere to go.
She had nothing to prove.

She just looked at the sky
and she dreamed up a dream,
whilst the milkman went off
in his float to sell cream.

It was later that day,
much warmer than most,
when the postman came round
to deliver the post.

"Rapunzel, Rapunzel, please let down your hair,"

called the postman from down on the bottom stair.
"You've got a brown letter. It looks like a bill.
Shall I leave it down here on the window sill?"

Rapunzel Curlytop
Terribly Tall Towers
Jabberwocky Way

Rapunzel just sat.
She didn't blink.
She had nothing to say.
She had nothing to think.

She looked out at the birds and started to frown,
so the postman just left it and went into town.

When the sun was full blaze, just after lunch,
the baker came round selling warm things to munch.

"Rapunzel, Rapunzel, please let down your hair,"

called the baker from down on the bottom stair.

"I've got a bad knee
but I'm not one to moan.
Let me send up some bread
and a hot buttered scone."

But Rapunzel just sat.
She didn't flinch.
She wouldn't move – not even an inch.
Not a sound was uttered.
Not a word was said.
So the baker went back to her shop to sell bread.

Now Rapunzel's aunt was the caring sort,
and round about four, some dinner she brought.

"Rapunzel, Rapunzel, please let down your hair,"

called her aunt from down on the bottom stair.

"I've made a fish pie for you to eat.
I've wrapped it in tinfoil to keep in the heat."

But Rapunzel just sat.
She didn't stir.
A statue wasn't as still as her!
She just watched as the rain began to fall,
whilst her aunt dashed off to the bingo hall.

Now this story must have a prince, of course,
and he showed up late, but not on a horse.
With the wind in his hair, and blowing his hooter,
along came the prince on the back of a scooter.

"Rapunzel, Rapunzel, please let down your hair,"

called the prince from down on the bottom stair.
He brought with him chocolates and roses red.
He wore leather trousers, and shades on his head.

But Rapunzel just sat – as still as a wall;
she didn't think much of her prince at all.
She just stared and stared and stared at the rain.
And the prince was never seen again!

It has to be said, without lunch or dinner,
Rapunzel was starting to get a bit thinner.

"To leave her without any milk was mean,"
said the milkman on hearing Rapunzel was lean.

"And I should have really delivered that letter."
(The postman felt guilty and wished she were better.)

"To think," said her aunt, "that she's all alone,
on the sixteenth floor, as thin as a bone.
Rapunzel has patience. She doesn't move.
She has nowhere to go. She has nothing to prove.
But to sit on your own all day and dream –
well, it's not really good for one's self-esteem."

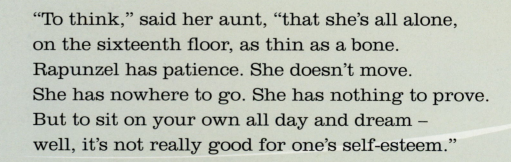

The milkman, the aunt and all of her friends
decided to gather and make their amends.
They climbed up the stairs – steady but sure –
all the way up to the sixteenth floor,
and burst through the door of Rapunzel's flat
(where she sat alone with only her cats).

They cooked her some supper, the first in weeks.
It brought the roses back to her cheeks!
The postman gave her the letter to read –
and what happened next, you'd hardly believe!

Rapunzel leapt up and she shouted with glee:

"I've got a new job at the library!"

She skipped round the room
and she started to groove.
She had somewhere to go.
She had something to prove!

She went to the cupboard
and brought out a spanner.
Then she fixed the lift
in a ladylike manner!

"Thank you, dear friends," she said,
"I'm all right."

So they all took the lift
and she turned out the light.

The following morning, at six o'clock sharp,
she jumped out of bed whilst it was still dark.

She tied up her hair in a very long plait
and pinned it all under a bright purple hat.

She put on a suit and a pair of smart shoes,
and ate a big breakfast whilst reading the news.

Then she got in the lift
and went down,

down,

down,

down,

to start her new job at the library in town.

Everyone loved her, she sparkled all day.
And life at the library continued this way.

For along with her hair and her ravishing looks,
she loved nothing better than **reading good books!**

Now Rapunzel has changed, and it makes her wince
to think that she used to just wait for a prince –
that she used to just sit, that she didn't move –
with nowhere to go and nothing to prove!

For **now** she reads three books every night
under the beam of her bedside light.

She can tell you the distance to the moon.
She can do Scottish dancing and
play the bassoon.

She can speak in four languages, skip and play chess,
she can knit tiny egg cups and cross-stitch a dress.
She knows the difference between crows and rooks –

and all because of ...

So don't just wait for your prince to show.
He might turn up, but you never know.
Pop down to your library and borrow a book –
there's **SO** MUCH to find out if only you look.

But don't just sit and wait and stare ...

when there's more to life than growing your hair!

ALSO BY WENDY MEDDOUR, PUBLISHED
BY FRANCES LINCOLN CHILDREN'S BOOKS

THE CINNAMON GROVE SERIES

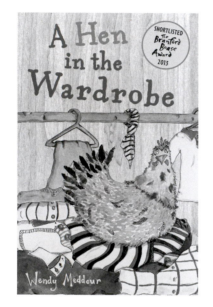

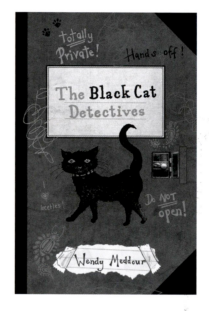

A Hen in the Wardrobe

Shortlisted for the Branford Boase Award

Chosen as one of the Diverse Voices top fifty
titles celebrating cultural diversity

The Black Cat Detectives

"A fast-paced, funny sleuthing adventure"
– *Booktrust*

"A highly entertaining, funny story
– *School Librarian*

Frances Lincoln titles are available from all good bookshops.
You can also buy books and find out more about your favourite titles,
authors and illustrators on our website: www.franceslincoln.com